Til Death Do Us Part

Stephanie Ayers

Til Death Do Us Part
First Print Edition
Copyright © 2013 Stephanie Ayers

ISBN: 0615922279
ISBN-13: 978-0615922270

Cover art and design © 2013 Jeremy Gann

Bannerwing Books
www.bannerwingbooks.com

DEDICATION

For my best friend, Shyla Flickinger, without whom the story never would have come to be.

For my loving husband who works hard so I can stay home and is my loudest cheerleader.

For my mom, my number one fan.

For my children who taught me the power of dreams.

For Wendryn, Marian, Carrie, David, and Jessie who all took the time to read, re-read, and edit while offering encouragement and support.

For Cameron and Bannerwing Books, the publishers of my story.

For my talented brother, Jeremy, whose fantastic artwork brought my story to life.

Without any of you, this book wouldn't be possible. Thank you.

Til Death Do Us Part

I.

The ring glittered from the small blue box, shiny and pure. An unstoppable smile worked itself across Ian's face as he thought about the ring's intended. His fingers caressed the smooth round stone absently as his mind sifted through memories, finally settling on the first time he really *saw* her.

Elizabeth sat at her desk, opposite a woman with mousy brown hair in a neat ponytail. The woman's lime green sweater was paired with cream-colored khakis. Trails of black lined her face, evidence of her tears. Ian felt pity for her though he did not recognize her.

"I'm so sorry, Caroline," Elizabeth said, a look of sympathy on her face. "We have no problem granting you a leave of absence."

Caroline nodded without smiling as fresh tears rolled down her cheeks and her fingers shred a tissue held captive in her hands. "Thanks, Elizabeth.

I really can't afford the time off, but I can't focus on work, either!"

Elizabeth stretched her arm out across the desk and placed her hand over Caroline's. Her voice softened as moisture filled her eyes. "I wish there was more we could do for you. No one should have to deal with the pain you are going through alone."

They rose from their chairs and Elizabeth embraced Caroline. "Keep me informed, and if you need anything—anything at all—please don't hesitate to ask."

A clear box sat on the counter top of the main desk when Ian arrived the next morning. Someone had taken time to craft a money mailbox. In neat handwriting, a placard above the box said:

Support a co-worker and support your troops!

Underneath, in smaller letters, someone had printed Caroline's name and revealed that her husband, an Army Sergeant, had been killed in Afghanistan. Only one check, made out for one-hundred dollars and signed in Elizabeth's elegant handwriting, graced the inside of the box.

Over the next few months, Ian noticed that Elizabeth always had a kind word and a ready hug for everyone she passed in the office. Any time a co-worker needed help, she always got involved.

Ian looked out from the second story window of his townhouse and his excitement grew. He remembered the first time he asked her to go on a

2

date. She had smiled at him as she stood in the human resources doorway.

"Um, Elizabeth, um..." His legs felt like they would collapse. "I'm umm... I'm Ian from the research department." He wanted to kick himself. Of course she knew who he was. He cleared his throat. "I, um, I hope I'm not, um, imposing, but... um... if you are free Friday evening, I'd, um, I'd like to take you out to dinner." He felt heat fill his cheeks.

Elizabeth smiled wider and said, "You know, I actually just had a cancellation, so, yes, I am free Friday night. What time would you like to pick me up?"

When she answered the door that Friday night, dressed conservatively in a rosebud pink cashmere sweater that set off her blue eyes and stonewashed denim jeans that hugged her hips, Ian realized he had already fallen in love with her.

He pulled the small blue box from his pocket and looked at the ring again. As the butterflies took flight in his belly, he glanced at his watch and realized that the company car would be coming around within the next half hour. He set the box on the counter. He still needed to shave and dress. Tonight required a clean look instead of his usual scruffy appearance.

The city-block-wide office building looked charming. Icicle lights dangled from the awning. Stickers displayed a North Pole scene in one front window and a manger scene in the other. Bing

Crosby crooned from the speakers as he walked through the spinning door. He smiled as he joined the party in the conference room. Cotton snow lay strategically around the dimly lit room. The boss served drinks from behind a portable bar. Silver snowflakes dangled from the ceiling and an empty dance floor replaced the long table and chairs that normally furnished the room. Many of his coworkers were already there, but his eyes searched the room for her.

Elizabeth Bunting stood off to one side, surrounded by men. Her long blonde hair haloed around her head, her ready smile commandeered your attention, and her blue eyes carried you away to paradise with a glance. Her sweet personality won everyone over. She was just as beautiful inside as she was outside, mostly because she had no idea how beautiful she really was. Ian was over the moon in love with her although they had only been dating for three months. He dropped his secret santa gift under the tree before casually working his way to where she stood and placed a firm hand on her back.

"Hi," he said in his shy way. She smiled softly at him.

"Hi," she responded, sliding her arm through his. He pulled her to the dance floor and they swayed gently to "The Christmas Song" as others filled the floor around them.

"I missed you." Ian murmured.

"I was only gone for a week." She laughed softly, and he wondered what was behind her mysterious smile.

"Yes, a week too long." He paused for a moment to look around the room. The party was in full force. The boss had given up mixing drinks, turned the bar over to a bartender, and was dancing with his secretary. His wife was dancing with one of the partners, a plastic smile plastered to her face. "Hey, what do you say we get out of here? Another ten minutes and we'll have been here long enough to be noticed."

"Give me thirty and I'll be ready."

"Fine, a half hour, but then you're all mine." He pulled her closer, drinking in the smell of her soft perfume, the feel of her body under his hands, the essence of her warmth pressed against him. "If things get crazy, though, we're leaving. Agreed?" He spun her as he spoke and she smiled.

"Agreed."

When the song ended, he released her. His hand went to his pocket and his fingers played with the small box hidden within it. This would be the longest thirty minutes of his life.

II.

"I'm ready," Elizabeth whispered in Ian's ear as they danced. They had mingled enough that the right people had seen them, taken time to gasp over their gifts in the appropriate manner, and now they were both ready to go. Ian helped her with her coat, taking a moment to appreciate the way her dress fit her body. He kissed her as they exited through the spinning doors, knowing no one was watching.

Despite the cold, the park was inviting. Someone had wrapped the trees in soft clear lights and added an archway at the entrance. Ornaments and lights throughout the park kept the magic going. Snow began falling again as they entered through the archway. Ian smiled. Tonight couldn't be more perfect, he thought. The appearance of the horse and carriage was timely.

"Shall we?" He smiled at Elizabeth.

"Oh, let's! I've never had a carriage ride before."

Excitement gave her voice a lilt. A hand popped out to help her step up and sit on the bench, Ian right behind her.

The driver laid a blanket across their laps and said, "Half hour for thirty bucks." Once Ian paid him, he hopped back to the front, and with a click of his tongue, the carriage moved forward with a gentle list.

Elizabeth moved closer to Ian, enjoying his warmth. "Oh, Ian! This night has been so perfect. I'm so lucky to be sharing it with you. Thank you!"

Ian's hand went to his pocket again and fingered the box. He remained silent as he put his arm around her and enjoyed the ride. He wanted to wait for the perfect moment. It arrived as the ride ended. With her hand in his as he helped her out of the carriage, he went down on one knee. The blue box appeared in his other. As her eyes watered, he released her only long enough to open it and show her the diamond ring inside. It was a classic Tiffany's cut, and it took her breath away. Her hand trembled in his. The small crowd around them stopped and watched as he removed the ring from the box.

"Elizabeth Bunting, you have no idea the effect you have on me. Every morning when I awake, I see your face in the sun. Every night before I go to sleep, I hear you whisper goodnight. You have given me a new outlook on life, and taught me how to appreciate the small things. You have given me so much... I want to spend the rest of my life making it up to you. Elizabeth Bunting, will you marry me?"

A collective "aw" swept through the air and danced among the snowflakes. Elizabeth was openly crying now, yet she pulled her hand from his. Her mouth moved but no words would come out. His eyes begged her to say yes as she looked into them. Their time together flashed through her mind like a slide show. She remembered the time they got stuck at the top of the Ferris Wheel. She had leaned forward as far as she could to see below them and he had visibly paled. She remembered the Italian restaurant where he wore more sauce home than he had actually eaten. Then a trip to the movies replayed in her mind. It was the premier of the latest Brad Pitt movie and the theater was packed. Only one seat remained and Ian had stood beside her throughout the entire three hour film. And then, inevitably, the memory she tried to avoid popped up. They had decided to drive across the bridge and another driver cut Ian off. Dismay filled her as she watched his face turn purple and heard the vile words that flew from his mouth. Her stomach lurched as his foot stomped on the gas pedal and tore after the other driver until he had followed him home, then got out of the car and punched the other driver. When he returned, she noticed the color of his knuckles rivaled the color of his face.

"All you have to say is 'Yes!'" someone shouted from the crowd, breaking her reverie.

"I... I... I can't," she fumbled. "I'm so sorry, Ian. I...I can't marry you. I enjoy the time we spend together. I enjoy your company, I really, really do. I'm just not...." Her eyes scanned the crowd quickly. Her voice lowered and her final blow came out in a whisper. "I'm just not in love with you. I'm sorry."

The small sound of shock from the crowd behind them made Ian stand up quickly. Tears filled his eyes as he turned and started walking away. Elizabeth reached out to stop him, but he walked faster, until he was running. The scene evaporated behind him as he disappeared down the path.

Once he felt he'd gone far enough, he took a moment to catch his breath and wipe the frozen trail of tears from his face. He was amazed to find the ring still in his hand and the blue box bouncing around in his pocket. He crammed the ring back in the box, and looked at it for a moment. It seemed dirty now, tarnished. His face melted in disgust, and he chucked it through the air, not caring where it landed. A deep sigh filled his chest and he released it. He collapsed on a nearby bench, buried his face in his hands, and gave in to his grief.

He did not notice the young man in the knit green hat stop his bike. He picked up the blue box and put it in his pocket, recognizing the trademark Tiffany blue. A smile that could chase black clouds away lit up his face. With his shoulders squared and his back straightened, his legs spun with renewed vigor as he rode out of the park.

III.

Vinnie locked his bike to the rack before entering the store. He was pleased to see there were no deliveries waiting for him.

"Can I take the rest of the day off?" he asked the man standing behind the counter.

"No. You know you're my only delivery person. Why would you ask?" Vinnie's grandfather asked in his heavy Italian accent. He always reminded Vinnie of Jim Carrey's character in Lemony Snicket's *A Series of Unfortunate Events*, tall and thin, with glasses perched on the lower bridge of his nose. He was a good boss, and he was right. Vinnie was his only delivery person.

"Because I found this in the park yesterday, and I wanted to see Sasha." He held out the open blue box and showed the old man the ring inside. "It's like a dream come true!"

"Boy! Do you have any idea the fortune that ring

cost someone? You need to return it to whoever lost it. Sasha don't need nothing like that."

"No, you don't understand, Grampa. He threw it away. I watched him. He just looked out over the bridge in the park and threw it. He didn't want it anymore, I promise. Please, can I at least call Sasha?"

His grandfather looked down on him with affection. "Such a lover you are." With a smile and a nod towards the back room, he caved. "No more than 5 minutes, mind you, boy!" Vinnie's back met his words.

"I know, I know!" Vinnie called back even as his fingers pushed the buttons they knew by heart. The line rang three times before a soft female voice came through.

"Hi. What are you doing?" His voice sounded as comfortable as he felt.

"I was sleeping." Vinnie could hear her yawn. "Are you working or just at the store?"

"I'm working. Do you still have class tonight?"

"Nope, I'm all done for the semester! I'm FREE!" Sasha squealed.

"Good. Can you meet me at the skating pond later?"

"Sure. I'll be there with my silver blades on."

"Good. See you tonight. I get off at five. And Sasha?"

"What?"

"I love you."

"I love you, too."

His eyes took on a dreamy haze as he began thinking about exactly how he would propose. He'd wanted to do it for a long time now, but never had enough money to buy a suitable ring. Sasha was a good, patient girl. The ring dropping at his feet at precisely that moment was a gift.

A dishtowel hitting his face brought him back to earth.

"Vinnie!" his grandfather said, laughing. He held a small bag in his hand. "I've only been calling your name for the past minute. Take this to Mrs. Amero over on 6th Street." Vinnie took the bag from him and started out the door.

Vinnie smiled, hearing his grandfather chuckle after him "Such a dreamer that boy is!"

IV.

Vinnie was glad that 6th Street was just around the corner. He'd forgotten his hat in his daydreaming and it was cold. Mrs. Amero would be disappointed. For as long as he could remember, she had always knitted hats for the Calzavara family. To his family, her hats were as sacred as the pope was. She would entertain him for a good 30 minutes at least, and he would probably end up with a new hat. It was her way. He loved being at her place during the holidays anyway. She had the best collection of Old World decorations he had ever seen.

He looked up as he locked his bike to a sign near the steps that led into her apartment building. A smile lit up his face as he saw the flickering rainbow of lights in her window. He could smell the fresh fruitcake and zucchini bread she usually baked drifting from the entranceway. He grabbed the bag, ran up the stairs, and knocked on her door.

"Vincente!" She exclaimed before placing a hand on either side of his face and planting kisses on both cheeks. She stepped back and looked him over. "Why are you so thin?"

Vinnie laughed. She always asked him this. "Because I don't get enough of your baking!" came his usual reply.

"And your hat?" She asked as she grabbed another from the coat rack and placed it on his head. This one was deep blue.

"Oh I ran out of the shop and forgot it, that's all."

She patted his face, pinched his cheeks, and smiled. "Well now you have two. Come, come. Sit." She fretted over him as he sat down at the kitchen table. She placed a plate in front of him full of various baked goods, all small samples, and a tall glass of milk. "Taste! Taste! What you like? Tell me!"

Vinnie did not hesitate. This was customary too, especially at Christmas time. He lifted each bite to his mouth and savored it as she looked on happily. "Mrs. Amero, yum. I'm supposed to choose from these?" He shook his head. "Impossible."

She clapped. "You are a good boy, Vinnie. Always know what to say. Take this back to your grandfather," she said, holding out a loaf of bread with a couple of bills laid across the top, "and tell him to fatten you up."

The early dismissal was uncustomary. He looked at her hard and, for the first time, he noticed the deep lines time had carved into her face. He noticed that she seemed a little more bent than normal.

"Are you all right, Mrs. Amero?"

"Tsk. Yes. I am as fine as an old woman can be. Now off with you, Vincente Calzavara." She escorted him to the door. He stopped just short of the opening.

"Mrs. Amero, can I ask you a question?"

"Yes, boy, but quickly."

He pulled the box out of his pocket again. Mrs. Amero gasped. She recognized the specialty blue. "I'm going to ask Sasha to marry me tonight. Do you think she'll like it?" The ring was all sparkles in the soft Christmas lighting.

"*Ma va là!*" she exclaimed in her native Italian. "If she doesn't, she's a fool, Vincente. *Mama Mia*, that's quite the ring! Any woman would be pleased. It's Tiffany's! Sasha's a good girl. She's lucky to have you. Oh! My boy!" She shrieked in excitement. She planted kisses and pinched each cheek again before pushing him gently out the door.

He looked at his watch, noted that it was almost 5:00 pm. He stopped at the deli long enough to confirm his grandfather could do without him for the rest of the day, and then headed back to the park. He wanted to practice his proposal because Mrs. Amero was right. He needed to do it right. Sasha deserved that after the five years she'd been waiting. He did not have much time.

The evening was early still and he was glad the skating pond was empty. A sign warning of the danger of thin ice went unnoticed as he entered from the street. The pond looked as frozen solid as it was every winter and smooth as glass. He did not need his skates. His rubber soles would keep him from slipping around too much as he paced.

He was so absorbed in what he was doing, he did not notice his surroundings. He did not hear the bells on the carriages as they pulled through. He did not see the park maintenance man picking up litter nearby. He was so lost in his thoughts he did not hear the ice he was pacing on cracking until it was too late.

The ice broke underneath him. He plunged into the water like a torpedo. The pond was deeper than he imagined and the cold hit him instantly. His legs and arms numbed almost immediately and his throat choked as the icy water flooded his lungs. His eyes locked on Sasha's, her face locked in helpless horror. One last breath sent a bubble to the surface of the pond, and he knew no more.

It had been a long day when the old orderly came across the bag of clothes left forgotten outside of the empty hospital room. He opened the bag and pulled out a still wet jacket. He felt a lump in the pocket and retrieved a water soaked blue box tied with a white bow. It opened easily enough and he gasped at the treasure inside. He looked around quickly. No one was watching. He put the box in his pocket and dropped the bag of clothes in the lost-and-found box, whistling as he went.

V.

The smile refused to leave Russell's face as he wrapped the blue box in green Christmas paper. He'd tried to provide a good life for his only daughter after her mother died, but life had been tough, and she spent far more time alone than he ever intended. He was proud of the woman she'd become; she was in college, living on her own, while working two part time jobs. This little ring would make her so very happy. He would give it to her this afternoon. Christmas was only a few days away, and there were more presents under the tree. He looked at the clock. She would be here any moment.

The door opened and she came in with a burst of chilly air.

"Dad?" Amanda called.

"Hi! I'm in the kitchen," he returned, wondering if she could hear his smile. He heard her keys drop on the cozy and the bottom of her heavy coat touch the floor.

"You sound happy." She stood outside the kitchen opening. Her black cocktail dress hung loose around her hips, the length shorter than he liked. Her light makeup made her look more grown up.

"I am happy! I have something for you, Manda Panda." He set aside the sandwich he was building and handed the small package to her.

He felt like a child in his anticipation. The urge to jump up and down was hard to resist but he managed. His eyes shone as she saw the ring. Her mouth dropped open and a light squeal crawled out of her throat. She pulled the ring out of the box and eased it onto the fourth finger of her right hand. She held her hand out, appreciating the rock that now decorated it.

"Oh my god, Dad! Oh my god! It's beautiful! I love it! Thank you!" She bounced across the kitchen and wrapped Russell in a hug, leaving lipstick on his cheek as she pulled away. Her smile sparkled all the way to her sienna eyes. She admired the ring again, holding it out for him to relish as well. He chuckled.

"It's beautiful, almost as beautiful as you."

"Oh, stop it, Dad. You're biased." Her flashing dimples told him she was pleased despite the blush that had crept across her cheeks. "Now, Dad, I need you to listen." Her smile turned serious and the dimples disappeared.

He sighed. There was always a purpose to her visit. She never stopped in just to see him unless it was a holiday.

"Yes, yes, Manda. I'm listening."

"I brought your new pills. They're in the bag on the cozy. There are two bottles inside. The white one contains your new pills. Dr. Gordon prescribed these if you start to feel a heart attack coming on. Do not take them for any other reason. Dad, do you understand? They could kill you if taken by accident." Her eyes searched his.

"I understand. Thanks for picking them up for me. You're such a good girl. What time are you coming over for Christmas?"

"I don't know yet. Mr. Kendricks said he needed some help in the store for a few hours and I could use the extra money. I'll let you know tomorrow, okay? I should go. I love you, Daddy. Don't work too hard tonight."

She put her coat back on, picked up her keys and shook the white bag. They hugged once more and he watched her leave.

VI.

A few hours later, Russell headed to the hospital to begin his shift. He was unaware that Amanda stood on a corner, only a few blocks over from the hospital. She'd switched her long coat for a short one, inched her too short dress up even higher, and replaced the black stockings with fishnet. She caught herself staring at the sparkle on her finger every time her hand caught a little light. Soon, a small grey coupe pulled up to the curb. A rough looking man sat behind the wheel. She smiled as she recognized him.

"Well, well. If it isn't Dougie Carter. I haven't seen you for a while. Looking for some fun?"

Yellowed teeth appeared between the dark stubble growing on his face. "Your rates still the same?"

"For you? Always." She flashed him enough leg when she sat in the passenger seat for him to realize she was naked under the fishnet. She giggled as she saw the rise in his pants. She was not attracted to Doug in any way, but he was a regular customer and a rather good one at that. Johns like him were hard to come by. She gave him the address of the hotel where she'd booked a room for the night and he drove off, one hand on the wheel, the other burying itself between her legs.

Her hands gripped the headboard. The mirror looking back at her reflected a mascara streaked face in the grips of ecstasy combined with pain as Doug slammed into her again. She knew what to expect from him, but tonight, he was impatient and unexpectedly rough in his urgency. He even brought out his special scarf, the one reserved for a specific frolic. She knew it was dangerous, but she got as much of a rush out of it as he did. She steeled herself for the final thrust before he released her hair and wrapped the scarf around her neck. He knew her too, and knew when she was reaching her climax. He always timed it perfectly, no matter how close he was.

Doug pulled it against her throat, lightly at first, letting the long soft silk caress her flesh. He was gentle now, his thrusts slow, a seductive dance between him, her, and the scarf. He teased her breasts with one end, then ran the other end of the scarf between her legs, tight and loose, until she gasped. He wrapped it tightly around her neck in the same instant that he rammed her again, pulling her head towards him, his grip on the scarf increasing the tension with each movement. Her body shuddered in response; her chest heaved as she struggled for air. He pulled tighter and tighter, his eyes closed, his face twisted in his own orgasm. As he climaxed, his arms twisted in the scarf, pulling it and Amanda's head tightly against his body.

Doug finished and released his grip on the scarf. Amanda fell to the bed in an unnatural heap. He panicked when he realized she was dead. He leapt from the bed, threw his clothes on, and hurriedly glanced around the room. A flash of light from her hand caught his eye. Breathing shallowly, he slid the ring off her finger, tucking the scarf back into his pocket. He grabbed the money off the nightstand and raided her jacket pockets. A small wad of cash was in one pocket, the blue box in the other. He took both and ran from the room.

Russell eyed the white bottle as he closed the door behind the police officer. Fresh tears carved new paths down his cheeks as he opened it and dumped half the contents into his hand. He stumbled to the kitchen where he absently poured himself a glass of water. He swallowed the pills one by one, until they were gone.

VII.

Dr. Drew Carter, freshly returned from a mercy mission overseas, had seen more than a lifetime's share of death. He did not need it here. The devastation of the Calzavara family had really gotten to him. He wanted to save lives, not watch them be wasted. It made no difference that he had done all he could to save Vinnie. He had been the doctor on call and it was his loss. He was still feeling the blow when he had to inform the janitorial department of the loss of one of their own, Russell. He'd taken his own life after learning of the death of his only daughter. It was a sad day around the hospital, and as long as people continued to trample each other over the best Christmas deals, it would continue to be a busy one.

His brown eyes closed as he inhaled. He did not realize he was holding his breath until his cellphone rang. It was his twin brother, Doug.

"Doug? This is not a good time." Drew knew his brother well and did not approve of his extracurricular activities.

"I know, man. It's never a good time with you." Doug snapped.

"What do you need?"

"I need $50.00." Drew heard the tremble of withdrawal in his twin's voice.

"No. I told you I wasn't giving you any more money. I'm not going to support your decision to ruin your body and your life, not to mention rotting your brain." Drew's shoes clicked loudly on the linoleum floor.

"Come on, Drew, it's Christmas. Please?"

"No, Doug, it's not Christmas yet. We still have four days to go. I'm not giving you money. I have to go. I have rounds to make, sick patients to see." Drew tapped the screen to end the call and pocketed his phone.

"Drew? Are you there?" Doug persisted, even though he knew his brother had already hung up. He slipped his phone in his pocket slowly before turning around. Someone was waiting in the alley behind him. He walked in a drunken stupor towards him.

"Hey, man. Look. I can't get it right now, but I swear I'm good for it." His eyes pleaded with the other man. Long dreads hung down his back and his business suit looked out of place with the multiple piercings on his face.

"Nah, man. My boss say you gotta pay. Nah

presidents, nah ice." His nose crinkled in a sneer as he watched Doug shake.

"Jai, you know I'm good for it. C'mon, man. Please? I gotta have some. I need it." He pulled everything out of his pockets. He had spent the $100.00 he scored from Amanda's pocket on some blow, but he had the ring. He pulled it out of the box. "Look, this is all I got. How 'bout you keep the ring for a deposit and when I get the rest of the cash, you give it back?"

"Ha. How 'bout nah? What I look like, a pimp? Nah presidents, nah ice."

Doug put the blue box back in his pocket and swung his right fist. It connected with Jai's left cheek and sent spittle flying. Before Doug could swing again, he felt a hammer connect with his face and an intense burn began in his abdomen. He was so close he could smell the garlic on Jai's breath, and he felt the blade slide upwards even as a hand stifled his scream. One final twist of the blade in his chest and he fell to the snow covered pavement. One corner of Jai's mouth lifted in a sneer as he took the box out of Doug's pocket and walked away.

VIII.

"Dr. Carter, we have a John Doe en route, set to arrive in exactly two minutes." The nurse behind the desk stopped him.

"Stats?"

"Male stabbing victim, been sliced up the middle. His heart rate is weak and he's lost a lot of blood. EMT says he's a mess." She looked at the sheet in front of her.

"Conscious?"

"According to the EMTs, no."

"Lucky man. Put him in three and send Gates out to get him. I'll swing around in a minute."

She nodded and went back to the board, adding Gates to Room 3. The phone rang and a patient came up to her desk at the same time. Drew walked away leaving her to handle it. His eyes caught movement coming from the ambulance bay. Gates was talking to the EMTs as they wheeled in a dark haired man on a stretcher. They disappeared behind a hastily pulled curtain. Drew breathed for a moment, sending a silent prayer up to God that he could save this one. His prognosis did not sound good. Perhaps there would be a miracle today. He watched the EMTs leave as he moved towards the room.

Gates was typing on the keyboard when Drew pulled back the curtain and entered the room. His eyes swept the familiar scenery while avoiding the lump on the bed. He wasn't ready to look at the patient yet.

"Vitals?"

"Poor. He needs surgery yesterday." Gates never beat around the bush. It was one of the things Drew appreciated most about him. He took a deep breath, fingering his stethoscope, and walked over to the bed. A guttural cry escaped his lips.

"Oh my God!" Drew felt his knees weakening. "Gates, please call Dr. Winslow, right now. I can't…I can't…" His breakdown frightened Gates and he ran out of the room. When he returned with Dr. Winslow, they found Drew more composed but crying, his fingers pinching the bridge of his nose.

"Dr. Carter?" they said in unison. Their concerned voices did not soothe him.

"He's my brother. I can't be his doctor. I can't. Please fix him. Please. He can't die."

Dr. Winslow immediately took over. "Gates, send in a nursing team and take Dr. Carter to the chapel. When you return, have them take him off the board until he is ready. We will cover his rounds." He reached out and laid a hand on Drew's arm. "I will do my very best, Drew. I promise. He is still alive and if I have any say over it, he will stay that way."

Dr. Winslow patted Drew's arm gently as Gates led Drew from the room. The chapel was empty. The blue walls were soothing, and classical music played softly.

"I'm sorry about your brother, Dr. Carter." Gates said before leaving him.

Drew's head dropped to his hands and his muffled cries filled the room. This could not be happening. He had spoken to his brother only a few hours ago. How could he possibly be laying in a hospital emergency room with his belly sliced open? It was not supposed to be this way. Guilt set in. He should have given him the money.

Oh God! Please God, please let him be okay. Please, Drew prayed.

An arm slid across his shoulders and he felt a hand grip his upper arm. The chaplain had joined him. Neither said anything, just sat there, as Drew continued to pray and cry, his body shaking with each sob, and the chaplain's hand on his arm providing some comfort. The shaking finally stopped, though the sobbing continued for some time. Drew lifted his head, raised his eyes to the ceiling, and rapidly blinked away the last of his tears. His head remained erect even as his eyes closed and a long heartbroken sigh escaped from his lips. He clamped his jaw and flared his nostrils as he breathed methodically. His breath came in jagged gaps as his teeth clenched and released, and water again filled his red streaked eyes.

The loud speaker sounded overhead.

"Calling Dr. Carter to the surgical unit. Dr. Carter to the surgical unit, please."

One last tug of emotion and Drew stood up. The chaplain tapped his back and stepped aside to let him pass. The surgical unit was two doors down and across the hall but to Drew it could have been miles away. Everything seemed distorted and stretched as he started down the hallway. White cloaked bodies were mere ghosts as they brushed past him, their movements unusually slow. A disembodied voice floated through the air asking him if he was okay. He ignored it, keeping his focus on his hand as it gripped the handle to the surgical unit and pulled. It would not open. He shook the door but it still resisted. The world came crashing back to reality like a jolt of lightning to a stationary tree, and he remembered that he needed his badge to gain entry. He held it in front of the sensor and the doors opened outward. Dr. Winslow was waiting for him.

"We patched him up, but he's got some really bad damage to one of his lungs and esophagus. He's very lucky that it missed his heart. I'm not going to lie to you. It's touch and go right now, but he is stable. He is still asleep, but you can go see him now."

Drew choked when he should have swallowed. His voice was hoarse as he spoke. "Thank you, Bennett." It was all he could manage.

Dr. Winslow touched his shoulder gently as he handed Drew the chart. Drew opened it and looked it over, his eyes misting with tears, before handing it back. He stared at Dr. Winslow for a moment, gave a small nod, and found his way to Doug's recovery room.

IX.

It was Christmas Eve and Elizabeth was excited. Her parents lived just outside the city but she did not have the opportunity to get away as often as she liked. She'd looked forward to spending time with her family for a few days. Her mind drifted to the memory of snow-covered lawns lit up with snowmen and reindeer, giant blowups of Santa, and glorious color flashing all over. She remembered the aroma of cider and cinnamon and cozy fires in the air. She wondered briefly what topper they had chosen for the tree this year. It was always something ridiculously glorious yet perfectly suited to her parents.

This was also the first year she would be going alone. She had no one to blame but herself. She could have invited Ian. She knew he would have accepted without question, but his recent proposal had put a stop to their budding relationship. She knew that she was not in love with him, and she had realized at that moment that she never would be. Her heart still belonged to another, though it was unrequited. She would not be able to love anyone else until she released him.

Traffic was the only thing that could put a damper on her Christmas spirit. The only way out of the water-locked city was by bridge. During the holidays, the bridge was always packed, and if you could travel more than an inch every five minutes, you were lucky. Today was no exception. An endless line of cars behind her matched the endless ocean of steel ahead. A slight jolt rocked her for a moment as an impatient driver bumped her fender.

She was beginning to regret taking the outside lane along the bridge as she saw big white flakes floating from the sky. Sudden visions of her car careening off the bridge, her body broken and bloodied, came to mind. She laughed at herself and shook it off, even as she felt a slight tremor come from the bridge beneath her. Another tremor sent the car behind into her bumper again. The jolt this time was a little harder, though still not enough to cause any damage. She inched forward as the traffic opened up slightly, wishing she were off the bridge already.

A few more inches and she could see the end of the bridge. The congestion was still heavy but she was relieved to see that it was at least moving. The bridge grumbled and trembled a bit more than usual and she would be more than happy to leave it. It was almost maddening in its noise. It slowly grew louder and she found herself at a dead stop. She imagined the little Rice Krispie elves standing on a rail and singing, "Snap! Crackle! Pop!" as the sound became significantly louder. A loud rumble that shook the entire bridge surprised and worried her.

The smell of hot steel filtered in through her vents as the bridge collapsed beneath her. Her trunk slid into the front windshield of the car behind, tossing her head against the seat. Glass sprayed her, some piercing her skin, as she came face to face with the bumper of the truck in front of her. Intense pain filled her even as she lost feeling from the hips down. Her eyes flicked around in agony. Her legs were pinned as the weight of the vehicles above crushed into hers. The bridge trembled again, shaking sideways as if blown by the wind. A small sound escaped as she realized with fading clarity that the vehicles were shifting and releasing some of the weight. The bumper slid to the left and the frame of her car lent support to the side of the truck as it turned. Her body was jarred once more and she screamed, but it was drowned out by the sound of the groaning steel.

Flashes of memory filled her mind—her fifth birthday party, her first middle school dance, graduation, and her first true love. His face came into focus before her. His clay-colored eyes surrounded by naturally soft skin; his easy closed lip smile that peeked from between two deep pits on either side of it and one just beneath it; his white doctor's jacket contrasting sharply with his healthy complexion. She heard his words again, hurting just as much now as they did then.

"I can't make you wait for me. It's not fair to you

or to me. What if I don't come back?" She remembered the weight of his hands on her shoulders. "What if I contract some fatal illness over there? I could never ask you to take care of me, to burden you in that way. No. It's better this way." She remembered the warmth of his palm cupping her chin. "We have no idea what the future will bring us. You know I won't stand in your way." She remembered the trail of tears on his face as plainly as if he were standing in front of her now.

Her voice bounced against the crushed frame of her car as she pleaded with him. "If you loved me, you wouldn't do this."

"That's not fair. You know I'm only doing this because I love you." He had reached out to embrace her but she'd pulled away, afraid of his touch, feeling his rejection. She still felt it, the aching pain that filled her heart now surrounding her body, suffocating her.

Her last memory was watching him get on the plane. He did not know she was there. She did not have the courage to tell him or to answer the phone when he had called until, finally, he stopped calling. She had lost him forever, and now he would never know. A whimper worked itself from her chest before her mind shut off, allowing her to fall into blissful darkness.

X.

"All doctors to the ER stat! Calling all doctors to the ER stat!" a panicked voice screamed over the PA system.

Drew raced to the ER. They'd all felt it. The television exploded in a volley of commentary as the local news stations began chattering on about the earthquake. It was an 8.6, the largest they'd ever had, and its epicenter had been just outside the city, to the south. The bridge had collapsed, buildings had crumbled, and there were multiple injuries. The holiday travel meant the count would be staggering.

All hospitals were on alert, and every doctor in the building, including the specialists, had come to help. Teams were put together to assist in rescues but Drew was not allowed to join them. They needed his expertise here. He said a silent prayer for all those who needed it and made quick rounds, organizing and moving patients as he went to free up much-needed space. When he stopped for a moment to catch his breath and soak in the enormity of what had happened, a pain seized his chest, sending him to his knees. In that moment, he knew Elizabeth was in trouble.

He pulled out his cellphone to call Doug before he remembered. Doug was recovering in a room upstairs. He glanced at his watch and then towards the ER desk. A few injuries were beginning to roll in. He knew he could not take off, but he had to talk to Doug, even if there would be no answer back. He needed to clear his head.

The elevator was moving too slowly so he took the stairs. The ICU ward was so silent that at first Drew thought it was empty.

"Dr. Carter? I'm surprised to see you here. All the doctors are down in the ER." A middle-aged nurse looked up from her clipboard as they passed in the hallway. He fell into step with her as she made her way to the nurse's station.

"Yes, I'm actually supposed to be down there, too, but I need to check on my brother for a minute. Do you mind?"

"No, but only for a minute." A small crack of the clipboard against the desk interrupted her voice. "He hasn't gained full consciousness yet, and his survival's still very fragile, as you know. Wait a sec?" She thumbed through some papers on the clipboard quickly. "Ah, yeah. It's actually a good thing you came by. He has some minor bleeding going on still and Dr. Winslow wants to run some tests. We needed your signature." A light appeared on the wall behind them. She pushed a form towards him. "Excuse me one sec?" She turned away as she responded to the patient's call. When she turned back, Drew noticed the weary expression in her eyes. This was not an easy ward to work on and her face reflected that. He handed the form back to her, all appropriate boxes checked, and his signature scrawled along the bottom. "Thanks, Dr. Carter. You can go in and see him now. He looks worse than he actually is, by the way."

"Let me know when they're going to run the tests, please?" She nodded, scribbled on a post it, and stuck it to the form. "I'll only be a few minutes then I'll be out of your way."

He moved quickly down the hall until he came to Doug's room. A soft whooshing filled the air as a machine pumped oxygen through Doug's nose. Neon green danced erratically across a screen above his head, dancing in rhythm with his heart rate, and wires flowed all around him like ropes anchoring him to the shore. Bruises decorated his face and faded away into the depths of a reckless beard. His disheveled brown hair was in need of a haircut. He looked like the little boy he'd once been, lost in the wires and blankets that covered him. Drew reached out and stroked his face softly.

"Oh man, Dougie, I need you. Please wake up. I… I think Elizabeth is dead. I can feel it. We had this major earthquake. A… a bridge collapsed, buildings came down, and I… I just can't help but feel something's wrong." His hand squeezed Doug's, and he longed for a return squeeze. "I know I was stupid to end it the way I did. I've never been able to stop thinking about her. Dougie…" His breath caught in his throat and his chest heaved. He drew in a deep breath and exhaled before continuing. When he spoke again it was in a whisper. "Dougie, what if it's too late? What if she's gone? What if… you're gone?" He choked over his last words. Faint pressure on his hand gave him pause and he watched Doug's face intently, full of hope, but his eyes never opened, his lips never quivered, and his lashes never flickered.

"Dr. Carter? I hate to interrupt but they are calling for you in the ER." It was the same nurse he'd run into in the hall. He turned to leave and she stopped him with a light touch to his arm. "For what it's worth, I hope your instinct is wrong." Her eyes searched his quickly. "About both of them." He rested his hand over hers for a moment before he released it and walked away.

XI.

The scene in the ER was messy. The injured were rolling in, overflowing the seats in the waiting room, and there were still more spilling out the door. He could hear sirens in the background and knew that more were on the way. His shift was due to end in less than an hour, but he knew he would not be able to leave as long as people needed his help. He still had to do penance for letting Doug down. Maybe this would be enough for him to wake up and live. He closed his eyes and breathed. He had to get Doug off his mind so he could focus on the patients. He gave himself a small shake and joined the others to take care of the endless sea of patients.

Four hours after his shift officially ended, the waiting room was still packed and the ambulance bay was just as busy. Rescuers were still working on the bridge looking for survivors. Drew wanted to switch places with some of those working on the bridge but the director refused to let him go. He was too valuable and the bridge was too risky. Aftershocks created more havoc for those working on the bridge, though there were no new injuries. He contented himself doing as much as possible to treat those he could and keeping those he could not fix comfortable.

He was taking a break in the staff break room when a nurse rushed in.

"Oh my God. Oh my God, it's awful."

Drew looked up from the magazine he was reading. "What?"

"They've broken through to the inner shell of the bridge where the more severely injured are, and they've started coming in. I… I'm not sure… how I am going to make it through… the rest of my shift." Tears streamed out of her eyes and sniffles punctuated her words. "I was out there, Drew. I was there. On the bridge. The first layer wasn't too bad. Injuries were minor. Then, as we worked backwards… oh."

Drew stood up and put a comforting hand on her shoulder. "I have confidence in you, Julia. You are one of the best nurses on staff. This is never easy. I'll see that you're removed from the bridge rotation from this point on if you want. I could use a second pair of hands."

Julia sniffled some more, taking another moment to calm down, grateful for Drew's presence. This was exactly why he was one of the nursing staff's favorite doctors.

"Please don't. If you take me out of the lineup,

someone with less experience may end up out there, and... that could be tragic. The last thing they need is someone inexperienced. I'll be okay. I just needed a moment."

Drew nodded. He understood exactly what she meant. Today was overwhelming and it was far from over. She poured herself a cup of coffee and drank it slowly.

"Why are you still here, anyway? Your shift ended hours ago."

"I couldn't leave. How can I? No one has left. Even those with the day off have come in to help. Besides, I have restitution to make."

"Restitution? For what?" She dropped her empty cup in the trash.

"Personal matters. I'll just say that I need to be here for my soul and leave it at that. I'm going back out. Take all the time you need." His smile was warm as he left the break room. He stopped by the desk to check on his patients, confident in his staff. The nurses behind the counter were a flutter of activity.

"Any new developments?" he stopped the one closest to him. She looked at the board quickly before responding.

"All staff is in attendance, either here or out there."

"Thank you, Janice. I am going to go assist at the ambulance bay. Who's on chopper duty?"

Janice looked at the board again.

"There are four ahead of you, but there are no incoming flights. There are two scheduled outgoing flights though. I'll buzz you when it's time. I should warn you that it's not pretty out there." Her head jerked in the direction of the ambulance bay.

"Thanks again. By the way, Janice, you are doing an incredible job. We'd be lost without you." He flashed that warm smile again. He had no idea what a soothing affect it had on all of them.

He strode out to the bay as an ambulance pulled up. The EMTs rushed out and threw open the doors, carefully but quickly pulling the patient out. He grabbed onto the cot and listened as they read off the stats.

"What happened to him?" he called to them quickly. Another doctor met them just inside the doors and took over, listening as they spoke.

"The crushed front and passenger sides of his truck kept him trapped on the bridge. His airbags possibly saved him from further injury. The lady in the car beneath his definitely got it worse."

His gut churned at the mention of a woman and his face dropped.

"Where is she? Is she en route?"

"They were still trying to get her out when we left. Look, I gotta get back out there." The EMT took pity on Drew and turned just before climbing behind the wheel. "She'll be here soon. This is the closest trauma ready hospital to the bridge."

More ambulances pulled up, some from the bridge, some from the city. Drew took charge of them all, directing where to put each new patient as they arrived. Some went straight to surgery, while others went to the ER. The halls filled quickly, and he realized that they would soon run out of room. He knew he should get back inside, but he could not. He would not be able to focus until he knew if the woman trapped on the bridge was Elizabeth or not.

"Dr. Carter?" An aide was calling his name. Drew looked his way. He did not know this guy. "You are needed inside, stat."

Drew frowned in confusion. He walked swiftly beside the aide.

XII.

"What's going on?"

"I'm sorry, sir. It's your brother. You are needed on the fourth floor immediately."

Drew's chin dropped as his mouth opened and his eyes widened.

"My brother? I was just there a few hours ago. My pat—"

The aide interrupted. "Your rounds are being covered. Go."

Drew moved quickly through the mass of bodies in the waiting room. He did not bother with the elevator and took to the stairs, two at a time, as he ran up. He did not stop at the nurse's station but continued straight to Doug's room. It was buzzing with activity and every nurse not helping in the ER seemed to be there.

His eyes flicked up to the monitor hanging from the wall. A small thin line ran straight across the screen. He was pushed roughly out of the way as two aides wheeled a defibrillator into the room. Tears filled his eyes as a pathway cleared and he saw his brother's ashen body on the bed. An angry thick line ran down Doug's abdomen where they had stitched him up. If they jumped him, his stitches would break open, but it was a risk Drew was willing to take.

"Do it!" Drew cried, moving towards the bed. A nurse stopped him before he could get too close.

"Let him pass," Dr. Winslow said and placed the paddles against Doug's flesh. He nodded and Doug jerked upwards and fell back to the bed, his neat stitches bursting open half way down the incision. The line danced shortly on the screen before settling back down to a straight line. Drew moved to the opposite side of Dr. Winslow.

"Again?" Drew requested. Another nod and Doug's body jerked upwards again before falling back to the bed, the rest of his stitches bursting open. All heads turned to the monitor, even as Drew grabbed Doug's wrist to check his pulse. Nothing. Drew heard a great sob fill the room. It took him a few moments to realize it came from him. Dr. Winslow looked at Drew with concern, tapping a nurse and sending her to Drew's side. Dr. Winslow looked at the clock on the wall.

"I'm calling it. Time of death 4:40 pm." Another sob filled the room. Dr. Winslow hung his head for a moment, allowing his eyes to close. The nurse remained at Drew's side. "I'm sorry, Drew. I did everything I could for him. His wounds were just too great. It's a miracle he hung on this long. Take all the time you need."

Drew did not hear him. His sobs were long and loud. Dr. Winslow instructed the nurse to stay with him until he calmed down, then he left the room. She backed off quietly, giving him room to grieve, moving closer only when he went to his knees and laid his head next to his brother. He closed his eyes, placed a hand in his brother's and just laid there. The sobs quieted, though he still whimpered occasionally. The nurse pushed a chair next to Drew and sat with him for a few more minutes before leaving the room. She slid the curtain closed and left him in peace.

The streets were quiet in the aftermath of the earthquake. A man slid in the door of the pawn shop just as the owner was getting ready to close. A blue box appeared in the palm of a hand, and the owner's eyes glittered. The box opened and the ring sparkled in the dim light. Greed was written all over the owner's face as he took out his eyepiece and examined it. He handed over a large wad of cash to the man and watched him leave. He replaced his eyepiece with a rag and polished the ring, making notations in a small notebook he kept under the counter. When he was finished, he slid it into a black velvet lined box and, with the lid open, put it in the front window display.

XIII.

In the same moment that Doug was giving up his life, Elizabeth was fighting for hers. As Drew was running up the stairs two at a time, she came in on a stretcher, oxygen bag attached, a doctor hand pumping it as they went. Someone had wrapped her mangled legs to contain the blood flow. Another doctor joined them as they pushed her towards the elevator. They were taking her to the ICU.

"This one's a fighter," the EMT pushing the stretcher said. "She's been in and out of consciousness even when she was still trapped in her car. It took the Jaws of Life to get her out. She lost a lot of blood. Her pulse is weak and thready. Her car is literally a tin can. She is very lucky to be alive."

"They've got the adrenaline you ordered waiting upstairs, Dr. Adams," a nurse said, joining them in the elevator.

They shared the stats as they exited the elevator. They wheeled her into a small room and quickly hooked her up to the monitors. Dr. Adams jabbed the adrenaline into her chest. A breath of a second, a tick of the third hand on the clock and her heart rate steadied and smoothed, though it was still weak. He barked out more instructions and the staff hustled around him. Nurses quickly hooked up bags of blood and medicine. Doctors filtered in and out of the room.

In another room not far from where Elizabeth was fighting to survive, a pager went off. Drew shot up, startled from the state of half-sleep he'd fallen into. Pain shot through him again as he looked at his brother one last time, then he covered him up and moved to the phone. He pushed the buttons on the pad that matched the code on his pager and listened to the voice on the other end. He sighed deeply, splashed some water on his face, and, without a second glance, walked out of the room.

The constant flow of staff in and out of another ICU room caught Drew's attention. His head turned in curiosity and a brief gap in the hustle left a wide-open view of the patient in the bed. He started to look away, when it hit him.

Elizabeth!

His stomach released a battalion of butterflies as it rose to his throat. His mind screamed her name. Heads lifted and eyes peered at him over their masked faces and he realized he'd shouted it aloud. Dr. Adams paused long enough to whisper in a nurse's ear. She quickly moved through the door, pulling the curtain closed behind her. Drew grabbed her arm gently as she passed.

"How is she?" His eyes sought hers earnestly.

"She is stable, that's all I can tell you. Are you a friend?" She did not know Drew. She'd seen him working in the ER and occasionally on the surgical ward. Most recently she'd seen him visiting his brother and she knew his brother had just passed. She wanted to give him hope, but did not have any answers.

"You could say that. Would you ask Dr. Adams to keep me posted? I have her contact information. I'm wanted down in the ER, but I'll be back when I'm done."

She nodded as he headed off, trying unsuccessfully to see into the room again. He was absentminded as he entered the ER but Janice quickly brought him back to reality.

"Those x-rays came back. Gates had some questions about them and since you are still listed as the doctor in charge and Watson has gone home…" She pushed a small pile of files towards him unapologetically as her voice faded away.

"Okay, I'll look through these. Have things been running smoothly?"

"Yes. They have been rotating well."

Drew's eyes scanned the waiting room as she spoke. Someone had gone through the room tending to as many injuries as possible while he'd been upstairs. They'd managed to organize them by groups too. He smiled.

"I'm going to make rounds and come back for these. By the way, thank you."

Her eyes fell but her smile widened. "It was the

least I could do, Dr. Carter."

He made his rounds quickly, pausing only long enough to make a dreaded phone call before going through the files. Dr. Winslow joined him shortly.

"Drew, why don't you go home? Most of these are fairly recent, and I have seen them all. I can take over."

"I can't. The patients need me."

"We're doing fine, I promise."

Dr. Winslow's hand on Drew's shoulder was both comforting and commanding. Drew's posture melted. He knew Dr. Winslow was right. He had Elizabeth on his mind anyway. He closed his eyes for a moment and sighed.

"You're right. I won't be far, so page me if you need me."

Winslow had dismissed him already, so he grabbed his arm and squeezed it to get his attention.

"I mean it, Bennett. Page me if you need me."

"Of course. Please, get some rest. I'm going to need your strength tomorrow. Goodnight, Drew." Dr. Winslow spoke to the air because Drew was already gone.

XIV.

Drew felt strange coming back to the fourth floor. Luck had not been on his side the last time he visited someone here. He was hoping for a better outcome this time. Elizabeth just could not die, especially now that he had found her again. The nurse behind the counter was new. She refused to let him see Elizabeth without Dr. Adams' consent. She ordered him out to the waiting room and picked up the phone to page Dr. Adams. He liked her no-nonsense attitude even though it defeated him. He needed more nurses like her in the ER.

He leaned his head back in an attempt to relax for the first time in what felt like forever. He had never been good at waiting, and, for the first time, he understood how patients' families felt as they waited for news. It had only been minutes but it felt like a lifetime.

Drew looked around the room. There were a few

others waiting with the same tired looks on their faces. A couple conversed in quiet tones on a lounge on the other side of the room. A young woman consoled a crying baby in the hallway. A man in a disheveled business suit sat opposite him. His fingers left paths through his hair. Rosy pink rimmed his bloodshot eyes. The splotches on his face gave further evidence of his tears. Drew wondered briefly who the man was here for when Dr. Adams came into the waiting room. He saw Dr. Adams acknowledge him with his eyes, but his lips bore greeting to the other man.

"Mr. McCullough?" Dr. Adams called out to the room.

"Yes? How is she?" the man in the business suit stood up.

"She is stable for now, but that could change any moment. She's lost a lot of blood. The surgery was successful in repairing her legs, but I'm afraid she may not walk again. The crash severed her spinal column. We did the best we could to fix it, even inserting steel pins, but it's up to her now. Have you been able to contact her family?"

The man groaned as he heard the news, dismay clouding his face. His head shook gently in response to the doctor's question.

"No. I..." he sniffed, "I don't have that information. Um, we..." he sniffed again, "we hadn't gotten that close yet."

"Hmmm. I'm sure her records are here somewhere. Does she go by any other name than Bunting?"

"No. She is single, unmarried." His response had

a touch of bitterness behind it that took Drew by surprise. He realized they were talking about Elizabeth and he rose to join in the conversation.

"Actually, Dr. Adams, I do have her contact information. I'm here to provide you with any information you need until her parents arrive. They live on the other side of the bridge, so they may not be here for some time."

Dr. Adams merely raised his eyebrows. "Was she a patient of yours?"

"No. She's my… She's a friend. We've known each other for a long time. I saw you working on her as I was leaving the ICU earlier. Her parents have no way into the city with the bridge collapse and request that you keep me updated on their behalf."

"I'll keep you updated as well as I can, Dr. Carter. Thank you." He turned to leave and Mr. McCullough stopped him with a swipe at his sleeve.

"And me? Will you keep me updated as well?"

The doctors exchanged a look before Dr. Adams answered.

"I'm not supposed to do that since you aren't family, but perhaps the good Dr. Carter will be so kind?"

Drew chuckled softly at the ease with which Dr. Adams had shifted the blame. He still did not know who this man was or what he meant to Elizabeth. That the man cared for Elizabeth was unquestionable, and Drew felt his heart sink. Perhaps he was the third party here.

"I suppose. I'm off duty so I'm not breaking any rules. She's not my patient in any event, so I guess I could do that. Mr. McCullough, was it?" He extended a hand out in greeting. The handshake was strong and yet unsure.

"Please, call me Ian. I, uh, I work with Elizabeth. Well, not directly, but in the same office. She must have listed me as an emergency contact. I left Christmas with my family to be here, so I appreciate this."

"Okay, Ian. I need to call her parents and update them with the news, so if you'd like to get some coffee or something, I'll make sure you don't miss anything."

"Thanks." He looked hard at Drew for a moment, debating on whether to trust him. "I think I'll, uh, take you up on that. I'll be back soon."

Drew breathed a sigh of relief. He wanted to see Elizabeth and having Ian leave made it easier. He followed Ian to the hallway, bringing out his cellphone and hitting speed dial before bringing it to his ear. He faked the conversation until Ian stepped on the elevator and the numbers began to light up.

He moved quietly through the ward. Dr. Adams looked at him from behind the counter, but said nothing. Drew found her room and pulled the curtain aside. Elizabeth lay on the bed, her eyes closed, tubes all around her, and the line on the monitor jumping steadily. He moved to the side of the bed where there were less wires and put his hand in hers.

"Elizabeth?" he whispered. Her eyelashes fluttered but did not open.

"Elizabeth?" he whispered again. "Squeeze my hand if you can hear me."

He waited, his heart in his throat, but she did not squeeze. Her eyelashes fluttered again, but still remained closed. She was pallid, the same ashen color Doug had been when he died. A small sob escaped his throat.

"Please don't die. Fight this. You can fight this! Please? I'm so sorry. I'm so sorry. I never should have let you go. Oh God, Elizabeth. Please come back to me!" His face crumpled as the tears started. He looked at her for another moment before the grief overcame him and he ran from the room, down the stairs, and out of the hospital.

XV.

The cold air sliced through Drew and astounded him. The sky was a solid mass of black, water pooled down the sides of the street, and the threat of snow clung to the air. Flashes of blue and red reflected from the water and bounced off the hospital windows. His steamy breath swirled about his head as he flipped his collar up around his face. He wandered without direction, down one street and up another, moving as far away from the hospital as he could stand before circling back around. He passed the same stores repeatedly, though only one caused him to stop and look.

It grabbed his attention as he passed on the opposite side. It was a mere glimmer, a catch of the streetlight in the shop window, but it aroused his interest nonetheless. When he crossed the street, it seemed to be calling him. It sparkled and glistened, a twisted flash of light with every other step he took. The handmade sign over the door simply said "Pawn" and yellow stickers revealed the name "Otto" on the door itself. Bars behind the door told him the shop was closed, though the sign still hung on open, and he could see a man milling around inside the shop. He took another step, landing him in front of the window. Jewelry of all shapes and designs sat in the spotlight but only one piece caught his eye. It was there, in the center, displayed proudly in black velvet, its stone centered and clear on its yellow gold base. He realized what he needed to do.

Drew tapped on the window and when the man looked at him, he pointed to the ring, pulling his wallet out and holding it up. The man met him at the door, fumbled with the keychain until he found the right key and unlocked the door. There was a strange smile on his face as he let Drew in.

"The ring? How much?" Drew danced from foot to foot as he waited for the man to pull the ring out of the window.

"Is genuine Tiffany. I have blue box too." He disappeared to the back room for a moment and returned proudly with the box in his hand.

The man moved too slowly for Drew's taste.

"Fine, fine. How much?" Drew pulled his credit card out of his wallet and shoved it at the man. "How much?"

"Hmmm. $10,000. Yes? Agree?"

"Yes. Run the card. Quickly, please?"

"You make some lady ver' happy." The man smiled widely, revealing the gap between his front teeth. "You make me ver' happy! Here go! Good luck!"

Drew heard the lock click behind him and saw the sign swing to "Closed." He stopped long enough to admire the ring once more before putting it in the box and pocketing it.

XVI.

When Drew went back to the hospital, he went through the main entrance. He did not want any distractions or anyone stopping him for questions. He went straight to the fourth floor and through the double doors. After a brief stop at the nurse's station, he entered Elizabeth's room.

There was a pallid cast to her skin but the rosy glow budding on her cheeks filled him with hope. He knew it would be a long night, but for the first time in weeks, he felt optimistic. A small smile worked its way across his face as he settled into the chair near her bed and promptly fell asleep.

"Dr. Carter?" the soft female voice sounded concerned as she shook his arm gently. When his eyes opened, she continued. "You asked me to wake you half hour before my shift was over."

"Ah, yes. Thank you, Kathy. Anything interesting happen?"

"No. However, that man? He's been asking to see Ms. Bunting. I didn't know what to tell him."

"Oh! Yes, I'll take care of it. Do you think you could let him come back for a little while?"

"Dr. Adams said no visitors. That's the problem."

A smile played at the corners of Drew's mouth. "Well, then I suppose you should respect the good doctor's orders. I'll go around, come in from the other side, and let him know how she's doing. Any changes?"

"Her heart rate's returned to normal and she's breathing on her own, but she still hasn't woken up yet. I really don't expect her to wake up for a few more hours anyway. She's been through quite a trauma."

"I agree. I have to go start my shift, but page me if there's any new developments or if she wakes up?"

Ian was a lump on the couch in the waiting room. If they were not there for the same person, Drew knew he would pity him. As it was, he decided to do the charitable thing and wake him up. Ian shot up, startled, before remembering where he was and why he was there.

"Elizabeth?" he asked.

"She's doing better. She should be awake in a few hours. Perhaps you'll get to see her then." Drew watched Ian's face fall and his heart softened. He realized this man was no threat to him, though he could tell how much he cared for Elizabeth. It was written in every line on his face, in the stubble that hid his features, and in his wrinkled clothing. "I'm sorry, Ian. It's hospital procedure. They will let you see her as soon as it's safe for her."

"Have you seen her?"

Drew's first instinct was to lie, and he did not understand it. He did not need to hide anything from this man. He cleared his throat to cover his discomfort. "Yes, I have actually. I stopped in a little while ago."

"How... how does she look? I mean under the circumstances?"

"She looks good. I think she's going to be okay. I really do." He watched as Ian's face brightened. "Look, I have to start my shift. Anyone on staff here knows me. Have them page me if you need me, okay?"

XVII.

Drew called to check on her several times during his shift, but there was nothing new in her recovery. With each passing hour she did not wake up, the weight of the box in his pocket grew heavier. His optimism was waning. The first chance he got, he went up to check on her. As he entered the room, her eyes opened. Her pained expression made it impossible to tell if she were trying to smile or grimace.

"Hi," he said.

"Hi," she answered.

"Should I call for the nurse?"

"No. I've been awake for a while."

His eyes turned to the floor even as his brows hunched together on his forehead. "Oh. I... I asked them to call me when you woke up."

Silence darkened the room and he felt his heart slow down.

"I know. I asked them not to bother you." Tears stung her eyes and she blinked, not wanting him to see them. She did not realize that he could still have this much of an effect on her a year later. His eyes dropped and her heart leaped but she ignored it. She was not going to allow herself to get all worked up over him again. She had bigger issues to deal with.

"Oh, I see. How are you feeling?" He did not see, though. His heart was in panic mode and threatened to burst out of his chest.

A wry laugh danced in the air. "I've been better."

"Have you talked to your parents?"

"Yes. They called a little while ago. They told me you called them. Thank you."

"Of course. Has, um… has Ian been in to see you yet?"

A small smile worked its way across her face.

"Yes. Poor Ian. I sent him home. It's Christmas. He should be home with his family. You know I'm going to send you home, too. You should be home celebrating Christmas with Dougie." She watched as emotions crossed his face and tears spilled over. He crumpled to his knees beside her bed. "What? What is it, Drew?"

"Oh God, Elizabeth. Dougie's gone. He's gone! He died yesterday. Some Christmas, huh?" The tears he had been holding back spilled over and ran down his cheeks. Anguished sobs escaped his throat.

Shock registered on her face as she tried to reach out to Drew and her arm would not move. An anguished cry filled with grief for Doug and for herself erupted from her throat as she remembered the accident again. The tears she had held at bay spilled over.

"What?! Oh, Drew. I'm so sorry. Oh GOD! Why can't I hold you! Ahhh!"

He moved his face to her hand and rubbed his stubbly cheek against it. Silence filled the room as they grieved together. After a few minutes, Drew stood up again. He reached out and wiped a trail of tears from her face. He looked deep into her soft blue eyes, allowing their warmth to carry him away. For the first time in a year, he felt like he was finally home.

"Oh, Elizabeth. I was so scared I was going to lose you, too. I have been such a fool. Such an idiot. I never should've let you go. It was the biggest mistake of my life, and now I'm scared it's too late." His head dropped down to his folded hands that enclosed hers. "Can you ever forgive me for my stupidity?"

Tears cascaded down her face as he reached into his pocket and pulled out the blue box. He looked at the clock on the wall above them. In less than a minute, Christmas would be over. He pulled the lid off the box, lifted the smaller velvet one out, and popped the lid open. A small gasp came from the bed. He sank down on one knee, still holding her hand.

"Elizabeth Bunting, I love you. The only future I see has you in it. Will you marry me?"

A smile broke through her tears. She looked at the ring sparkling in the bright fluorescent light as he slid it on her ring finger.

"Even if I never walk again?"
"Even then. You are my life."

ABOUT THE AUTHOR

Stephanie Ayers spends much of her free time living in the alternate universes created inside her imagination or from the pages of another's. When she's not writing, she mothers her 4 children, loves her husband, attends church, and neglects housework as often as possible.

Connect with Stephanie online:

http://frommywriteside.wordpress.com
http://www.facebook.com/theauthorSAM